THE NYACK LIBRARY
NYACK. N. Y 10960

P9-APX-053

THE SEVEN FLORA McFLIMSEY BOOKS

Miss Flora McFlimsey

and the

Baby New Year

881266

BY MARIANA

THE NYACK LIBRARY
NYACK, N. Y. 10960

Lothrop, Lee & Shepard Books   *New York*

ILLUSTRATIONS BY MARIANA RECREATED BY CAROLINE WALTON HOWE.

Text copyright © 1951 by Marian Foster, renewed 1979 by Erik Bjork.
Illustrations copyright © 1988 by Erik Bjork.
All rights reserved. No part of this book may be reproduced or utilized in any form or by any means, electronic or mechanical, including photocopying, recording or by any information storage and retrieval system, without permission in writing from the Publisher. Inquiries should be addressed to Lothrop, Lee & Shepard Books, a division of William Morrow & Company, Inc., 105 Madison Avenue, New York, New York 10016. Printed in the United States of America.

Second Edition   1 2 3 4 5 6 7 8 9 10

Library of Congress Cataloging in Publication Data
Mariana. Miss Flora McFlimsey and the Baby New Year.
Summary: Miss Flora McFlimsey has a surprise late night visitor on New Year's Eve. [1. Dolls—Fiction   2. New Year—Fiction] I. Title. PZ7.M33825Mfp 1988   [E]   86-15339
ISBN 0-688-04533-2   ISBN 0-688-04534-0 (lib. bdg.)

It was New Year's Eve.

Miss Flora McFlimsey was sitting before the fireplace in her little red rocking chair.

All the other dolls had gone to a party in the Big House, but somehow Miss Flora McFlimsey had been forgotten. She was feeling rather lonely, so she had come downstairs to sit by the fire and watch the Old Year out. Pookoo Cat was asleep on the hearth rug.

It was cozy and warm in the dollhouse, but outside the wind howled and blew the sleet against the windowpane. Pookoo Cat stretched himself and sat up.

"Why don't you make some good resolutions for the New Year, Miss McFlimsey?" he asked.

"Yes," said Miss Flora McFlimsey, "I suppose that would be a very good idea. Are you going to make some too, Pookoo?"

"Certainly not," answered Pookoo. "I don't need to. I'm always perfect. I wash behind my ears and no mouse is safe when I'm around—except, of course, Timothy Mouse, but that's only because he's a friend of yours."

Miss Flora McFlimsey looked uneasily toward Timothy Mouse's corner. Pookoo gave his head a shake. The little bell on his collar went tinkalinkalink.

"No," he said, "there's no reason why I should make resolutions, but it's different with you, Miss McFlimsey. Now, I don't like to mention it, but do you remember that evening last June when you hid under the lilac bush while everyone was looking for you so that you could brag to the other dolls that you'd stayed out in the garden all night?"

"Yes," answered Miss Flora McFlimsey humbly.

"And that night before General Jackson's birthday party when you pinned your hair up in curl papers so you'd look prettier than Genevieve?"

"Yes," whispered Miss Flora McFlimsey. She was dreadfully ashamed of that. The little girl in the red-topped shoes had found her hiding behind the piano and had scolded her and brushed her hair out straight again and put her little black hair ribbon back on her.

"But the worst thing you did," continued Pookoo, "was when you promised Bo-Peep you'd look after Baa so she could go to the picnic in the Pine Forest. You were so interested in listening to that silly bird singing out in the apple tree that you forgot all about Baa. That gave *me* a chance to pull him around and chew his ear."

"Yes, I remember..." said Miss Flora McFlimsey.

She was silent for a little while, then she asked rather timidly, "Didn't you jump up at the Christmas tree, Pookoo, and knock some of the balls off and break them?"

"Why, yes," said Pookoo. "But I should not have done that. I should have climbed the tree instead and shaken it. Then all the balls would have fallen off at once."

"Oh," said Miss Flora McFlimsey.

Pookoo Cat lay down again and closed his eyes. Tick-tock, tick-tock, went the clock.

Miss Flora McFlimsey stared at the fire. She thought of Baa and little Bo-Peep, and sighed. This year she'd try to be better. She'd keep her promises. She wouldn't envy Genevieve her curls anymore. She wouldn't fall off the piano stool when she was put on it to practice her music lessons. She'd learn her ABC's. And she'd try to be kind.

Miss Flora McFlimsey sighed again. Perhaps she'd better go to bed after all. It was lonely sitting there making resolutions and listening to the wind.

She got up and lit her little candle and tiptoed over to
the stairway.

But what was that? Pookoo jumped to his feet. Could
it have been the wind? It came again. This time it
sounded like a little cry. Pookoo was walking around the
room waving his tail.

Could there be someone over in the shadows crying?

Suddenly, with a loud WHOOSH! the door blew open. The snow swirled into the room, and blown in with it, like a feather on the wind, was a tiny creature with dimpled arms and legs. It had no clothes on, only a ribbon tied over one shoulder.

"Oh!" cried Miss Flora McFlimsey, putting down her candle and running toward the little shivering thing.

"Look, Pookoo! What is it? Is it a doll? Is it an angel?"

"His name is written plainly on that ribbon," said Pookoo, "and if you'd learned your ABC's as you should have, you could read it. It says LITTLE NEW YEAR."

Miss Flora McFlimsey put her arms around the little creature and tried to lift him. He was heavy, but somehow she managed to carry him over to the fireplace.

Then, still holding him, she climbed back into the rocking chair.

Pookoo curled himself up again on the rug. "And just as I was having such a nice nap," he grumbled. "My mother never left us kittens around on doorsteps to come blowing in and waking everybody up on cold winter nights. If we wandered off, she went after us and brought us back by the scruff of our necks and gave us a good nip on the ear besides."

Miss Flora McFlimsey didn't seem to hear him. She was bending over the Little New Year, rubbing his tiny hands and feet and whispering in his ear.

"If only I had something to put on you," she said. She thought for a moment. Then she carefully laid the baby New Year down on the rug and went over to the trunk. There, in the top tray, was a wee shirt. She hurried back with it. It was rather hard to get the Little New Year's arms into the sleeves, but at last she succeeded and buttoned it up.

"You must be hungry, too," she whispered. She went over to the little cookstove and poured some milk into a saucepan.

When it was warm she poured it into a tiny cup and gave it to the Little New Year to drink.

Just then Pookoo opened one eye. "It was bad enough," he said, "to wake me up, without taking the milk intended for my midnight supper..."

Miss Flora McFlimsey wasn't listening. She was rocking the Little New Year and singing a lullaby. She could only remember one line of it:

> "When the wind blows,
>   the cradle will rock,"

but she sang that over and over.

She didn't feel sad or lonely anymore. She felt wonderfully happy. She had even forgotten about the party in the Big House.

The Little New Year fell asleep and Pookoo slept again. Miss Flora McFlimsey kept on rocking and singing in her tiny voice, and the clock ticked on.

At last the Little New Year stirred. He opened his eyes and smiled. At that moment the clock struck twelve.

Then, quite suddenly, he seemed to grow bigger, and in another moment he was gone! He slipped out of her arms, the door blew open, and he ran out into the night.

Miss Flora McFlimsey ran after him, but the door blew shut again.

"Oh!" she cried. Then all at once she was back in her little rocking chair before the fire. Bells were ringing—bells near and far away.

Miss Flora McFlimsey rubbed her eyes. Had she been asleep? Could it have been a dream? She walked over to her trunk and looked in the top tray. The little shirt was gone!

She stood still a minute listening to the bells. How beautiful they sounded! Over in the Big House she could hear people calling "Happy New Year!" Someone was singing:

> "Should old acquaintance be forgot
> And never brought to mind?
> We'll take a cup o' kindness yet..."

Miss Flora McFlimsey didn't hear the rest of the song because just then Pookoo came over. His little bell was ringing too—tinkalinkalink. He put out his paw. "Happy New Year, Miss Flora McFlimsey!" he said.

NYACK LIBRARY   NYKL

2827 00696 2805

JP
MAR   Mariana

HOLIDAY   Miss Flora
          McFlimsey and the
          Baby New Year

831266

$10.88   p

	DATE		
4/98	8	8/99	J.S.

THE NYACK LIBRARY
NYACK, N. Y. 10960

© THE BAKER & TAYLOR CO.